dilitirio

a novella

Timur E. Simsek

dilitirio

Thriller

Editorial: Debra D. Stout

Printed and published by BoD – Books on Demand,
Norderstedt, Germany

ISBN: 978-3-7578-1788-6

Observe the world and it'll tell you the truth

O N E

Welcome to Milos!

A small island in the Aegean sea, a place some might consider the holy definition of paradise. An almost mythical oasis where the light blue ocean was in stark contrast to the dark and heavy clouds. It was late summer and the temperatures were mild, so rain was unlikely to come by any time soon. Evenings could be spent out on the patio drinking white wine and eating fresh fruit. Milos was one of those few places still untouched by modernity or tourism. It was the true Greek experience. Men playing backgammon in narrow alleys. The smell of fried pepper everywhere. Rugged, grayish-white mountains defining the shoe-like island. With its shallow golden beaches, turquoise see-through water, and white-blue houses, it presented plenty of unique landscapes. Milos was one of those places you could just let go of all your worries. Well, almost...

"Tragedy struck Milos today when farmer Akis Marakos stumbled upon a woman floating dead in the Papafragas caves" – as was reported by a news announcement later that day. Akis owned an apple

farm close by and he was planning on taking his lunch break on one of the cliffs after collecting his harvest all morning long. He had been eating there for the past thirty years, and today would be no different. Akis was a round, stocky man in his early fifties. He had eyes going opposite ways and thick, white whiskers, looking much like the men during the colonial ages. He was a beloved member of Melian society and considered by many to be the kindest man on the whole island. The caves were his favorite thing in the world. The chalk-colored cliffs and the light blue-green water were one of the most beautiful sights he had ever laid eyes upon. Already as a child, he would look down into the caves at the small rocks shimmering on the bottom of the ocean. Or he would try to count the amount of tiny fish swimming around. Upon sitting down that morning to eat lunch, expecting to see nothing else but water and pebbles, Akis glanced mindlessly into the water. Suddenly, he recoiled in shock when he saw something sinister before him in the deep. It was a naked woman floating face down in the clear water, her body whipping from side to side in the faint waves. Without thinking twice, Akis immediately notified emergency helpers. While anxiously waiting for first responders to arrive, Akis' lunch crashed down on one side of the cave and then catapulted into the water underneath.

To no one's surprise, Aki's disturbing discovery sent shockwaves through the tiny island. Never before had the islanders seen such a horrific thing. Certainly, there had been people dying occasionally, and now with the Melian mafia splitting into two parties there was more violence, but the islanders considered themselves to be civilized people. Leaving a naked woman floating dead in such a beautiful location seemed almost a sin. It was decided by first responders that the unknown woman should be transported back to Adamantas, the largest city on the island so that forensics could take a closer look at her demise and possibly put a name on her.

Meanwhile, Inspector Dionisis Lagos was in Mandrakia, enjoying the taste of wine and the company of beautiful women. Somewhere in the background, a TV was making noise. Mandrakia was on the northeast side, right at the coast and roughly a ten-minute drive away from Adamantas. Lagos' family had been living there since the dawn of time. The city was a small collection of colorful houses, all with direct access to the sea. Each house had its own fishing boat, oftentimes matching the color of the respective house. It was in one of those buildings, the village tavern to be precise, where all guests could hear Lagos' roaring laugh echoing through the rounds as one of his many lustful women gently tickled his neck with her playful kisses. Indisputably, he was having the time of his life. "There are only two things every man must truly love; wine and women", Lagos said laughing at a young man sitting not too far away. The guy looked at him in a rather awkward way. "Probably a tourist. Doesn't know how to enjoy life", Lagos said to the woman sitting on his right side. She had been busy caressing his chest hair, so when he suddenly addressed her, all she did was nod. "Someone bring more food!", Lagos shouted at one of the waiters. It didn't take too long for a young man to bring fresh fruits, Saganaki - fried feta, cheese, olives, watermelon pie, Ladénia - the Greek version of focaccia, and some pita bread seasoned with salt and thyme.

"Tragedy struck Milos today when farmer Akis Marakos stumbled upon a woman floating dead in the Papafragas caves".

Upon hearing that statement coming from the TV, Inspector Lagos shot up from his comfortable spot so abruptly, the women jumped. Lagos intensely stared at the TV screen and listened. The news reporter talked about how Akis had sat down to enjoy his lunch when he found the dead body of an unknown woman floating down in the caves. "That's not good", Lagos said sternly to himself. He had a dark foreshadowing. Just as expected, suddenly his phone started buzzing. Sullenly, Lagos picked up and said: "Yassas, Dionisis Lagos speaking". As expected, it was his superintendent. After a minute or two of receiving instructions,

Lagos ended the conversation with: "I'll be there shortly". Then, he hung up the phone and looked at the women. "I must leave. There is business to be taken care of". The women seemed genuinely disappointed for him to leave but knew they couldn't do anything about it. Lagos had been ordered to come to Adamantas.

While the inspector was driving to Adamantas, Valentina Zehnder returned to her hotel room after jogging along Achivadolimni beach for the past hour. She usually didn't go for runs, and certainly not for that long, but she had this venomous urge plaguing her. Valentina was extremely agitated and had to move her body to get her mind off of things. Her worries lay with her best friend, Stefanie Sigmund. The two of them were Swiss tourists and they had been spending the past two weeks peacefully on Milos. Enjoying nothing more but each other's company and the warm weather. Unfortunately, after having a small argument earlier this morning, Stefanie had stormed out during breakfast, never to be seen again. It was now early evening and Valentina was frightened that something bad had happened to her best friend.

"Why don't we go to Greece?", Valentina had suggested roughly a month before Stefanie and her would board a plane to Milos. "That sounds like a fantastic idea. I haven't been to Greece in forever",

Stefanie had replied. She wore a big smile on her face when her dark brown eyes met Valentina's grey ones. Appearance-wise the two best friends couldn't have been any different. Stefanie had brown, straight breast-long hair that she oftentimes wore in a messy bun. Her skin was pure silky-white perfection. Her body was tender and slim apart from her behind. Her buttocks were what drew most men in. Valentina on the other hand had red, short hair and lots of freckles. She was also of slim build but with neither noticeable breasts nor butt. Oftentimes, her sickly looks made people stay at least three feet away from her. But it was all right. Valentina didn't care much for men. She was more than happy with Stefanie getting all the attention. Unlike Stefanie, Valentina didn't like being the center of attention. She was more of the observant and silent type. She saw and knew everything, oftentimes being underestimated by her peers. Stefanie had her heart in the right place, but she only cared for superficial things like fancy cars, big houses, and men with status or money. Her goal in life was sitting pretty at the beach and drinking fresh coconut milk while shy men shot timid looks at her. Valentina enjoyed the company of books and intellectuals. She loved people with whom she could have deep and meaningful conversations. Yet, even though the two girls seemed like complete opposites, that might have just been the reason why it worked. Valentina and

Stefanie had met in their first year of high school. Like so many true, and honest friendships, theirs was created out of pure coincidence. They sat next to each other during their first class, and upon noticing common interests, they decided to stick together. Six years had passed since, and not a single day had gone by without the two girls talking to each other. Later, upon finishing and receiving their degrees, they decided to move in together to save money. Traveling to Greece had not been their first vacation together, but one that was badly needed. Valentina had been working like a mad person and desperately needed to take a break, while Stefanie wanted to get away for a little while. Just a couple of weeks prior had she broken up with her latest boyfriend, who was now bothering her at every opportunity. Deciding to flee the country, and perhaps meet a "handsome Greek god with olive skin, green eyes, and curly hair" down south, seemed like just the right thing to do.

So it happened, just a couple weeks later, that Valentina and Stefanie boarded a plane headed toward Athens. After a short, rocky flight they touched down in the land of myths, colors, and heat. Before long, the two girls were on a ferry out to Milos. Upon arriving in Adamantas, Valentina and Stefanie hailed a taxi to take them to their hotel. The check-in went smoothly and soon enough, the two were standing in their cozy, little hotel room. "Don't they offer soap? What is this

place? Oh my god, and the bed squeals too?",
Stefanie shouted to Valentina, who had just
hoisted her suitcase onto the bed. In true Swiss
fashion, the first thing her friend did was complain
about something. There was always something to
nag about. It wasn't that the Swiss didn't
appreciate what they had, but instead it was to
advise anyone and anything on how to reach
perfection. Good isn't good enough. Perfect is. With
that mentality, any Swiss walked through life. Just
like a hand-made watch had to run without error,
so too had life to unfold in a pristine pure state of
perfection.

After a short moment of settling in, the two girls
went for a short exploration walk. They always did
that whenever traveling together to locate the most
important stores, such as the beauty salon, the
Italian restaurant, the groceries store, and the
pharmacy. After that, they decided to lie a bit on
the beach, where Stefanie eagerly checked the
scene for boys. Apart from some middle-aged hairy
men with pot bellies, no prince charming was
around. But not all had been lost. Above everything
else, getting a tan in was equally as essential to
getting boys as having your nails done. Tanning
was especially important to the rather pale-looking
Swiss people, who loved nothing more than to just
lie in the sun like dead flies. "God, I've missed the
sun. Valentina, I'm telling you, sometimes I get
depressed at home", Stefanie exclaimed. "Tell me

about it. I was born in the wrong country. I belong at the beach", her friend replied while casually turning on her back. "Promise me, these two weeks will be the best of our lives", Stefanie said while taking off her sunglasses so she could throw Valentina a worried look.

"I promise".

While the two Swiss girls enjoyed the sun, Helena Kostea was hanging out at her villa. Wearing nothing more than a bathing robe and holding a glass of champagne in her left hand, she lie on a deck chair out on her balcony. From there, she could see almost one-third of the whole island. She had just finished a business meeting and was now ready to bask in the sun. Right as she was about to take a sip, a young handsome man stepped out onto the balcony. He had dark straight hair and fierce green eyes, as well as a well-maintained beard. "Came to declare your undying love for me?", Helena said playfully.

"I'm sure that's what you would like to hear".

"So it's not true"?

Helena made a face as if she had been shocked. With her long, black, curly hair and black eyes, Helena knew she was considered to be one of the most beautiful women on the island. She was slim but with a noticeable chest, something especially alluring to men. "You're left to find out", the man replied. "I like your confidence", she said while looking away from him and out into the landscape. "I did not come here to just play games with you". Helena returned by saying he shouldn't act like he didn't enjoy their "daily business", which was her synonym for sexual intercourse. "There are other, more pressing concerns at hand", the man said and an air of seriousness came over him. "Like what"? Helena was genuinely getting annoyed by his forcing the conversation. "Perhaps the split of our company? In case you haven't noticed yet, we now have two separate parties. Us, the Achillian Party, and then the Hectorian League led by your uncle", the man said in a pressed way. "I am well aware of the split. But don't worry my love, we will still get what we're after". With that, she got up and put a hand on his shoulder, then she added: "You'll see..."

On the south end of the island, a sweaty and exhausted young man by the name of Joey Lewis returned to his large mansion. He had been out on a search all day long. Unfortunately, he had been unsuccessful, and accordingly, his mood wasn't cheerful. "Good afternoon, sir", an elderly man said upon his arrival. "Hello, Monty. Thank you for opening the door", Joey said as he stepped inside. The mansion lay on a large estate owned by the Lewis family for generations. Joey's ancestors had moved to the island in the early 1800s. They had always been considered novelty, especially since the Lewis were known to be an old British family. Decades ago, the house had multiple servants in their employment, but now, all that was left was a single butler called Monty. Monty had been an old friend of the family and even when money was short, he had stayed around. Joey considered the old man to be a person of honor and saw him as a close friend and ally. Monty usually ran the whole house, which consisted of multiple wings, a garden with flowers, a fountain, direct access to the ocean as well as a large veranda, from which Joey had just entered. "By the look on your face, I take it the search was a failure?", Monty enquired. "Yes. Another dead end. I'm not sure I will ever find this damned apple", Joey admitted, after throwing his shoes off and laying down on the divan. "Don't give up hope, young sir". Monty smiled at him. "Shall I make you a daiquiri to loosen up the nerves"?

"Yes, make it two. I want you to have a drink with me, Monty".

"As you wish, sir".

The house of Lewis had been in financial crisis for the past seven years. Ever since Joey's father had died and the son had gambled away most of the fortune. Joey knew he was a cunning, handsome young man, but he was also lazy and addicted to gambling. These rather undesirable traits, as his mother would always say before her passing, had let him to search for an ancient artifact apparently hidden somewhere on the island. In his father's room, which was the office ever since the house had been built and therefore held plenty of old documents, Joey had fumbled upon something peculiar. The apple of Hephaestus. Unfortunately, this relic worth billions had been long lost and most islanders doubted its existence. But, Joey was hopeful.

He would find it and restore his family's legacy.

T W O

"I will put you on this new case", the chief of police explained. Dionisis Lagos sat in his boss's office, across from a big-bellied man with a grey, pompous mustache. "You mean the girl who was found floating dead in the Papafragas caves?", Lagos inquired as he lit a cigarette. He had hand-rolled it only a few seconds prior. "Precisely!" his boss said.

"Why? There are plenty of other capable young men out there who would love the opportunity".

"Because there is something to be figured out! It cannot possibly be a random coincidence for a young woman to just turn up dead one day on this island. Especially a tourist, if one were to believe the rumors".

"What are you implying?", asked Lagos as he let out a fume so big it momentarily hid his face. "We must know if she is in connection to our mission - ". While saying that, Lagos' boss looked at him in a way that had his counterpart understand immediately what had been meant by *our mission*. "- and for that, I need a man I can trust. A man with experience. A man, like you". The supervisor leaned back into his leather chair. Understanding the importance of this assignment, Lagos asked: "What would you have me do"?

"Go to the forensics office and figure out who the woman is, what she was doing, and most importantly... what caused her death"!

It was roughly half an hour later, that Inspector Lagos entered the forensics office in Adamantas. It was busy with men in white plastic suits hurriedly walking from one end of the room to the other.

"Inspector Lagos, it's good to see you". Lagos was greeted by a young, somber-looking man with curly brown hair and a well-maintained beard. "Yassas, Selim", returned Lagos.

"I reckon you're here to see the woman found at Papafragas"?

"As always, you're reading my mind". The curly-haired man smiled. Lagos and Selim, a young Turk originally from Adana, had been close companions ever since the latter had moved to Milos a couple of years ago. Severely overqualified, Selim had quickly built himself a reputation as a respectable pathologist. The man was barely older than twenty-five and yet already considered to be one of the greatest minds on the island. While Selim led Lagos into a dungeon-like room, he said: "She is in here, ağabey". While Selim turned on the light, Dionisis looked upon the dead body. It pained him greatly to see such a beautiful, young woman laying lifelessly on such a cold table as this. Death had given her the paleness of a blank sheet of paper. There were no marks or any other indication of harm on her body. In her untouched purity, she almost looked like she had been induced by a deep slumber.

"Do we have a name on her"?

"We do, but it was difficult to come by. She was found completely naked and thus without any sort of identification on her -". Lagos interrupted Selim by asking: "Were her clothes not close by"? Selim shook his head. He then continued his story:

"A receptionist working the hotel she was staying at, saw the tragedy on TV and called in to assist us in this case. The name of the victim in front of you is Stefanie Sigmund, a Swiss tourist. She was vacationing on the island with her friend Valentina Zehnder".

Lagos was surprised by this revelation. Who would go around killing tourists like that?

"What else did the receptionist say"?

"That's it, ağabey. That's all she could give us".

Lagos nodded. "What's the cause of death?", he asked, as the two men looked upon the nudity of the corpse. "We're not certain yet. At this point, we can't even say if she has been the victim of foul play, suicide, or a mere accident".

"Can you keep me posted"?

"Certainly. You'll be the first to receive my report".

Valentina and Stefanie sat at a table placed directly

on the beach of Pollonia. From there, they could observe the light blue-green water of the ocean. The sun had been settling for the past twenty minutes and thus the sky had taken the color of deep-purple and pink. Small clouds graced the scenery. The heavens were contrasted by the earthy color of the beach. While the girls waited for their starters to come, they could hear the moored boats crack as they swept over the soft rippling waves. In the distance, the rough mountains laid the grounds for the white houses with their colored porch columns. Galíni, the restaurant chosen for tonight's dinner was well attended, but there were also plenty of residents going about their business. "I never want to leave this place", Stefanie said dreamily. An orange-colored cat started snuggling around Stefanie's leg when the waitress placed hard cheese and filled wine leaves on their table. The two girls had been exploring the island with a rental car and then decided to have dinner. Eager for new experiences, they made sure to order local dishes. "What is that?", Valentina exclaimed as she frowned upon the oily wine leaves.

"Looks like a turd of some sort".

"Come on, now. Try it first, before you deem it disgusting", encouraged Stefanie.

"You're right".

Stefanie was always right. She was continually open-minded, and kind. Valentina liked her a lot, especially because Stefanie pushed her out of her comfort zone, something Valentina struggled with often. Valentina admired her friend's spirit of adventure. Together with a fine bottle of Greek wine, Gemista and Pitarakia were served. Both the food and the wine were outstanding. It didn't take the alcohol long to unleash its full potential and get the girls tipsy. While the two friends had an in-depth conversation about their food, a young man entered the restaurant. Stefanie noticed him immediately and could not take her eyes off him. Never before in her life had she seen such a man. The word beautiful wouldn't even come close to describing his divinity. Like a god amongst mortals, he made his way to the bar, where he seemed to be ordering something before turning around and letting his mesmerizing eyes wander across the crowd. "Valentina, don't be too obvious but check out the guy that just walked in", Stefanie whispered to her friend without taking her eyes off the stranger. Trying to be subtle about it but failing miserably, Valentina flung back her head and saw a sweaty man, partially covered in dirt. He had blonde, flat hair and the face of a child. He wasn't particularly tall or athletic. He was a mediocre man at best. With a look of disdain and unhappiness, he leaned against the counter of the bar. "I don't get it. What am I supposed to see?", Valentina asked. "He's beautiful. I'm going to go talk to him", Stefanie said. Valentina was shocked. That was far from typical Swiss behavior, especially for women.

Most of the time, it was their job to just sit pretty and ignore the male presence until no further avoidable. To just get up and go talk to someone seemed so bold, so outrageous. "Are you drunk?", Valentina inquired. "Drunk with love at first sight, yes", Stefanie said sarcastically and got up. In disbelief and with a feeling Valentina could only describe as anxiety, she watched as her friend made her way over to the bar. What had gotten into Stefanie? Ever since they had gotten onto this island, her bestie was a new person. Gone was her timid friend. Who was this newly born creature of lust?

With a feeling of envy, Valentina sat alone at her table and watched Stefanie talk to the stranger. They seemed to hit it off immediately. Deep down, Valentina had hoped the man would reject her friend and just shoo her away. Seeing Stefanie having the courage to actually go talk to the men she found attractive, weirdly pained Valentina. Stefanie was flirting so blatantly, it was almost awkward. But he seemed to reciprocate. Suddenly, and to the surprise of Valentina, Stefanie waved her over. As Valentina drew closer, she could hear the man say: "I'm Greek, but my family is originally from Britain". Upon noticing her friend, Stefanie said: "Valentina, meet my new friend! This is Joey -" Valentina threw a fake smile of sympathy at him and he returned it equally as shallow "he's originally from Britain but his family has been living on the island for ages now".

"Pleased to meet you". The only thing colder than his smile was his hand.

"Nice to meet you too".

"Joey here has invited us to his house party tomorrow night", Stefanie explained. She was beaming like the sun. Valentina looked at Joey with a mixture of surprise and intrigue. Feeling her suspicion, he said: "That's right! I'm hosting some of the most important members of the island tomorrow and it would be my greatest honor to have two such beautiful ladies attend", Joey explained, his eyes moving from one girl to the other. Upon receiving no answer from Valentina, he added: "My estate is on the south end of the island. Trust me, it is worthy of the Swiss standard of prestige". Stefanie's begging eyes made Valentina give in. "We'd love to join", she said and smiled. "Delightful! I must leave now for I have urgent matters to attend to, but I will see you tomorrow", said Joey, and with that, he said goodbye to the ladies. The two of them watched as he and his evening coat fluttered out of sight.

"Isn't he charming?", Stefanie asked as they returned to their table. "Looks and acts like an imposter, if you ask me", Valentina returned.

"Don't be like that now. Trust me, this party will be fun. How many times in life do you get the chance to attend a high society event on Milos"?

"I just hope we don't get murdered and left in some dodgy alleyway".

THREE

"I have nothing to wear!", cried Stefanie. Valentina was getting ready in the bathroom. As she was applying mascara, her friend appeared behind her wearing a red, elegant dress.

"Looks good to me", Valetina said nonchalantly.

"Stop lying to me! It makes my hips look awfully chubby".

"Put something else on then".

"If you were a man, what would you love to see me in"?

"No clue. My personal favorites are black, red, and navy blue".

"You're no help!", Stefanie whined and then stomped out of sight. Valentina had purposely mentioned the only three colors her friend ever wore. She understood well why her friend acted the way she did. Tonight, they would attend Joey's party and the stakes were accordingly high. Stefanie hadn't talked about anything else the whole day. The young man had clearly possessed her very being. The two girls had spent most of their afternoon at the gym, getting a sweat in and working out their bottoms as much as they could.

Valentina didn't like working out as much. She never fully understood the excitement someone could get out of repeatedly lifting metal pieces in a room full of sweaty, cocky wannabees. Stefanie on the other hand could never fully grasp why Valentina didn't put more effort into her body. In her opinion, the reason she never got any action, was because she didn't care enough about her appearance. Eating too much sugar and being fond of fatty food paired with never going to the gym was just not a good combination. The two of them were not thirteen anymore. A Red Bull for breakfast affected the body now. Valentina, in Stefanie's opinion, had never been to the gym consistently enough to see any decent progress and that's why she never got into it. Once understanding the benefits of fitness and seeing how much a gym pump can boost self-perception is like a drug. Not only does it increase confidence, it simultaneously works as a motivator to return the next day. Something, Valentina never experienced. With her grubby dress, Valentina was prone to get no man once again tonight. Stefanie on the other hand was set out on a mission. Joey had been on her mind ever since she first laid eyes on him the other night. She was already head over heels for that boy. During lunch, she had imagined herself at Joey's side living together on his royale estate. Their two children, George and Diana, playing tag in the gardens. Their lives would be splendid and untouched, floating aimlessly through a universe of consonance and deep passion.

Once Valentina was done in the bathroom, she stepped out to see Stefanie laying on the bed. She was clearly day-dreaming about her prince charming. Stefanie was crushing over Joey, which left her worried. For some reason, Valentina got a bad vibe from him. She was skeptical of his over-the-top generosity and hospitality. There must have been an underlying reason for his doings. But, there was also another deeper issue at hand. Valentina was secretly infatuated with her friend. She hadn't told her best friend and never planned on doing so, but seeing Stefanie fall in love with someone else hurt her deeply. Probably because it would eventually lead to the two friends living separate lives. Being replaced by a man at some point stung like nothing else.

Some time later, the two girls were picked up by a chauffeur, personally sent out by Joey. "We're being carried away to paradise like they used to do in the old days of decency", Stefanie said dreamily as she got into the black G-Wagon. "Or like pigs sent to the slaughterhouse", Valentina remarked cynically. Speaking their native Swiss-German dialects, the driver could not understand a single word that was being said. In absolute silence, he drove them to the Lewis estate. While driving over and coming down from a small hill, the mansion started appearing in the distance. The respectable grounds astonished both Valentina and Stefanie. From the mansion, with its different wings, emanated a ray of golden light. At least two dozen gas lanterns shed their dim lights into the darkness of the night. From afar, the two girls could see glamourous women in their elegant dresses strolling about in the gardens. Men and women alike seemed to talk about all sorts of topics in the most subtle and civilized manner, while gazing at the different flowers and fountains. Pulling up into the parking spaces, both girls were nervous when stepping out into the mild, late-summer night.

The interior of the house was plastered with exquisite paintings and drawings. Some of the most renown artists had made it into the Lewis estate. Vases stood decadently on marble pillars and flowers of elegant colors graced the hallway. When the two girls entered, Joey was talking to a beautiful woman in a short, black dress greatly flattering her baffling physique. As if he had felt their presence, his head suddenly jerked around to them. With a big smile and his arms wide open, he approached them. He was closely tailed by the woman he had just talked to. "I am so glad you could make it. My party is now complete with you both being here", Joey exclaimed. After welcoming them by name, he said: "Looking lovely, ladies. I am beyond thrilled to host you in my humble establishment. Food and refreshments can be found all around, so do help yourselves. But before you wander off, may I introduce you to a dear friend of mine". Joey then drew the attention of the girls to the woman in black. "This is Helena Kostea. Helena -" he let his arm wander elegantly "- these are my friends from Switzerland, Valentina and Stefanie". "It's an honor. I've never made the acquaintance with someone from a country so respectable as yours", Helena said and smiled. "And I have never met a woman more beautiful than you", Stefanie returned the pleasantries. Valentina agreed. Helena started blushing while thanking them. What her friend had said was true. Helena was truly a treat to the eye. With her gorgeous black hair and the same colored eyes, she mesmerized anyone coming close. With her breath-taking physique and sharp intellect, she turned men into stone. Helena was the Medusa of modern times. After some minutes of benign talk, Valentina noticed Helena whisper something into Joey's ear. While Stefanie was rambling about the paintings, Valentina listened in on what Helena said. "Let's have a moment in private". With a slight nudge to the left, Helena indicated what she meant by that. Joey nodded understandingly. In hopes of not making it too obvious, he continued their small talk before saying he had to attend to other guests arriving. A grand excuse, but one Valentina took only too gratefully. Stefanie could not be pulled away from him anymore. "How about you ladies go have some drinks and I come to catch up with you later"?

"Certainly", Valentina agreed and with that pulled her friend away. Clearly disappointed in not being able to continue orbiting his presence, Stefanie marched through the hallway with her head held high. Out on the porch, overlooking the gardens, the two girls started chatting with other people. They met a couple of forgettable people before Valentina excused herself to go to the bathroom. Leaving Stefanie alone, she went back inside, where she took a left turn and started wandering down some hallway. Making a right turn eventually, she stumbled upon Helena and Joey. Hiding behind the corner, she watched as the two of them entered a room. The way they giggled and hung at each other indicated a certain activity to happen soon. As they got out of sight, she heard Helena say: "We need to talk. It's urgent"! Intrigued and spontaneously deciding to eavesdrop, Valentina crept up to the room, to hide behind a bush. What she saw, shook her to the core.

FOUR

"I went out looking for the apple again, but my search was fruitless", Joey said frustrated. Helena could tell how disappointed and stressed out he was. "We must find it before someone else does", she said. His frustration slowly swept over to her. She didn't mean to be angry with him but he had repeatedly failed her at this point.

"I know that! It's just, whenever I read the documents and apply them to the map, a new location reveals itself to me".

"Then you've got to go look in those spots. What do you want me to say"?

"You think I don't do that? That's why I keep going out on these day-long searches".

"Listen, Joey. I'm more than glad this team - she said it with a slight unidentifiable undertone - is nice and all... but I need results". After quickly pausing, she added: "You know what will happen if you should fail". With her air so suddenly and seamlessly changing, Joey's heart sank. Helena's look of cold calculation and ruthlessness made even Valentina's skin crawl. Never had she imagined such a lovely lady to have such a cold and menacing demeanor. She was right outside the door and it was only thanks to her fable knowledge of Greek that she could follow along the conversation. "The apple of Hephaestus must be on Milos somewhere! You and I both know how priceless it is. Once found, the apple can restore your family's wealth and establish the Achillian Party as the predominant rulers of this island", explained Helena as a look of dark greed came across her eyes. "That is what you want, don't you"? Having said that, she drew closer and started caressing Joey's face. Only seeing his back, Valentina could not make out his facial expression. What on earth were they talking about? What was this apple of Hephaestus? Who or what was the Achillian Party? Valentina wasn't aware of Joey's financial troubles, but she sure made note of it. Her eyes widened once she saw what happened next. With a wild passion, the two of them started making out, before Helena threw Joey onto the bed. Slowly going down on him, she started orally pleasing him. Valentina watched with a feeling of arousal as Joey suddenly started using Helena's mouth with passionate violence. They quickly went over to having equally untamed sex as the foreplay. While she was riding him, Helena said: "Bring me the apple and I'll give you the world. Fail to do so and I will end -". Joey's hand abruptly shot up and grasped her neck so strongly, it prevented her from finishing the sentence. With a feeling of having seen enough, Valentina wanted to creep quietly away, but she failed miserably when she clumsily fumbled over the strelitzia, which had provided her with cover. Alarmed by the noise, the pair on the bed suddenly stopped dead in their tracks. "What was that?", Helena asked. "Who cares", Joey replied and with a movement of incredible power, flung her around so he could be on top. What happened after that, Valentina would never know. She didn't particularly care either. Her mind was preoccupied with this mysterious apple and whatever the Achillian Party was. Sunken into deep thought, she wandered back out onto the porch in an effort to find Stefanie. There were urgent things to be discussed.

Dionisis was at home trying to sleep. But it just wouldn't come over him. His mind kept circling around Stefanie Sigmund. What an injustice to have lost such a beautiful woman so early on in her life. For reasons he couldn't explain, he considered it his upmost duty to find out what had happened to her. Never before had he such a feeling for any of his cases. Most of the time, he didn't care much. He had become an inspector because his father and his father's father had been one. Dionisis Lagos never cared much for police matters, let alone for actually solving other people's problems. He had his own issues to worry about. Nonetheless, he did appreciate the status and wealth that came with being an inspector. Especially out here on Milos. Lagos could get away with almost anything. Nothing ever really happened, so no one doubted his skills. But now it was different. People expected him to step up. They wanted him to be the hero he had proclaimed to be.

Lagos was originally stationed in Athens but due to his severely poor performance with the police force there, they had sent him away to this island. Banishing him into exile. Here, he had acted as if back on the main land he had been the best of the best, and for that reason now owned the great honor of serving the Melian people. Having an unexplained death on the island suddenly put all eyes on him. People expected him to solve this case. For reasons he couldn't even explain to himself, he wanted to oblige. Perhaps it was Stefanie's beauty, the fact that she was foreign, or the tragedy of her sudden death that moved him so much. Lagos was certain if it had been any other random islander, he wouldn't have cared nearly as much. Rolling from one end to the other, he tried falling asleep when suddenly his phone rang. "Yassas, Lagos speaking", he said with a hoarse voice. "Merhaba ağabey, this is Selim. The forensics report on Stefanie Sigmund just came in. Can you come by the office right now?", said the voice on the other end of the speaker. "I'll be there shortly" and with that Lagos hung up and flung himself out of bed.

Shortly after, he walked into the forensics office which was completely deserted this time around. Only a small, dim light was shining in the back somewhere. Under it, young Selim sat stooping over what appeared to be a document of some sort. Disturbed by the noise, the young man suddenly jerked his head around. Once laying his eyes on Lagos, he said: "My friend! Glad you could make it". While shaking his hand and simultaneously leading him back into the dingy room, the place where Stefanie Sigmund's corpse lie, he added: "What I have to show you is of upmost importance"! "On the phone, you said you have Ms. Sigmund's forensic report"?

"Indeed, ağabey".

While Lagos once again went over to the dead body to look upon her, Selim went to a table at the back end of the room, where a couple of scattered files and papers lay. As soon as he had found what he was looking for, Selim started reading: "Over the course of the last twenty-four hours, the body of Stefanie Sigmund was recovered and brought back to Adamantas. Dr. Arman and his team began the investigation ordered by the Grand Jury into the death of the twenty-three-year-old female. An autopsy has been performed and a toxicology report written. From these efforts, it can be concluded that Stefanie Sigmund's primary cause of death was drowning. However, the toxicology report found a high dose of cyanide in her blood stream. Her manner of death is henceforth determined to be accidental". Understanding that this must be a lot to take in, Selim watched silently as Lagos processed the information.

"Wait, so you're telling me she accidentally drowned? Like, she just fell into the caves and simply couldn't get out"?

"It's a possibility, yes. But get this, ağabey, the high amount of cyanide indicates that she either overdosed or was poisoned before falling into the caves".

"What can you tell me about cyanide, Selim"?

"It's a naturally occurring chemical that is widely used in the field of medicine. Low levels of cyanide are unharmful to the human body".

Lagos fell into a deep silence.

"My friend, cyanide is extremely hard to come by. It leaves only the possibility that she must have a prescription for it", Selim explained and with that stepped closer to the inspector to look him in the eyes.

"That's why they determined her manner of death as an accident"?

"Indeed. There isn't sufficient evidence to support a homicide. The way it's looking right now, it all points toward a tragic accident".

In the darkness of the room, whose only source of light was the full moon shining in from the outside, the two men looked into each other's eyes, deeply emersed in thought. Both of them silently agreed, that this was neither an accident nor a suicide. But how could they prove otherwise?

FIVE

Inspector Lagos spent the rest of the night at home, researching cyanide. But, it didn't turn up anything useful or new. The next day he spent canvassing all drug stores and pharmacies in Adamantas and the surrounding areas. Not a single one sold drugs or prescriptions containing the toxin. It was mind-bending! How on earth had Stefanie gotten her hands on such a nostrum? If it wasn't her, who had poisoned her? And how did they get a hold of it?

The next morning, frustrated and in desperate need of clearing his head, Dionisis Lagos drove out to the Papafragas caves. For some reason, he was hoping to find something out there. Deep down, in his very gut, he had a feeling he might stumble upon a possible clue. An answer to this conundrum, because clearly, he was missing something. He had to see the full picture to understand what had truly happened. While he was driving to the caves, minding his own business, he looked upon acres and acres of apple trees. It was that time of the year when they were ready to be harvested. It was close to noon when

Lagos arrived at the caves. As always, Akis was having his lunch on the edge of the cliffs. They greeted each other and exchanged a few words. The old man still seemed deeply disturbed by the gruesome find he had made. "I hope you bring her justice soon so she may rest in peace", Akis said before getting up and climbing onto his tractor. "I hope so too", Lagos replied. He waved the friendly farmer goodbye and then sat back down.

After a little while of just looking at the water beneath, he suddenly heard hushed voices. It was a man and a woman. They seemed to be bickering about something. Not trying to raise any suspicion, Lagos just sat silently without moving a muscle. The man and the woman slowly climbed out of the caves. To his surprise, Lagos recognized the pair immediately. It was Helena Kostea and Joey Lewis. She, the cunning head of the Achillian Party, and him a rich deadbeat who had fallen from his grace. The Achillian Party had recently split from the Hectorian League, and ever since, two warring mafia parties had been causing a lot of havoc on the island. Seeing her here was not a good sign! Hence, Lagos was not too keen on interacting with her. He asked himself what the pair was up to. He started walking over to them. Lagos could see their tensed-up faces. They were clearly not eager to see him either, which made the inspector chuckle a little to himself. Once he was close enough, the inspector opened the conversation with: "I see you have picked a side, Mr. Lewis". "What is it to you?", Joey sneered while making a face of great hubris, like the entitled little prick that he was. Lagos made efforts to inquire into why the two of them were loitering around the caves. He was met with a coldness so harsh, not even the most northern parts of the world experienced it. "Are we not allowed to swim here?", Joey growled, purposely acting even more stupid than he actually was.

"I didn't know you could swim, Mr. Lewis".

"Why are you here, Lagos? Trying to find the apple?", Joey said arrogantly and with an air of looking down on him. "Firstly, it's *Inspector* Lagos to you. Secondly, I care incredibly little for the affairs of the mafia", replied Dionisis. "You might not like it, but you're part of the Hectorian League just like the rest of the police force. Perhaps you don't care about their business, but you sure do want to find the apple. Not necessarily for the benefit of the League, but certainly for your own greed", Helena said with curled lips. "That's rich coming from the woman owning half of the island. Out of all the people here, you are probably the most likely to use the apple for your own advances", replied Lagos cooly, before adding: "As I said; I've never cared much about myths and legends, but what I do care about is a naked woman turning up dead at Papafragas. The exact caves, you two just crawled out of". Clearly understanding what the inspector implied, the pair just looked at him silently. Apparently done with their little conversation, the two of them walked past the inspector and toward their car. Before getting in, Helena turned around and said to Lagos: "Tell my uncle I said hello".

"Stefanie! Stefanie, you've got to come with me!", Valentina said hysterically. Stefanie, who had been waiting patiently on the porch of Joey's estate, was remarkably confused. She had been enjoying herself during this lovely social gathering. Stefanie had even met some interesting people. "Why? What's wrong?", she asked. Valentina was in a frenzy. "We have to talk! But not here, somewhere more private", Valentina ushered. Understanding that something was wrong, Stefanie merely nodded and then followed her friend back inside. The pair walked down the large hallway, then took a right turn and went up a flight of stairs before entering a room that appeared to be an office of some sort. There were bookshelves on all sides of the room and right across from the door, a large window made it possible to look down into the gardens, and out into the ocean. A large dark-red, wooden desk occupied the center of the room. A leather chair stood adjacent. Not paying much attention to where they were, Valentina pulled Stefanie in, shut the door, and then nudged her to take a seat on the desk. "What is all this about?", Stefanie asked. She was starting to get anxious by her friend's peculiar behavior. "I just happened to witness something", Valentina started but then suddenly, she got quiet. For some reason, she seemed to be contemplating whether or not it had been a smart idea to let Stefanie in on this knowledge. "Come on then, Valentina. Spill the beans"!

"You're not going to like what I'm about to tell you".

"I don't care. Just tell me already".

"Promise you won't be mad".

"I promise".

"I saw Joey and Helena having sex".

Silence seemed to have slapped Stefanie across the face. Confused, and visibly hurt, she said: "You saw what"? Valentina just nodded reassuringly.

"This can't be".

"It's true. I would never lie to you. But, they were also talking about something else".

"Like what"?

"About an apple of Hephesus or something like that. I couldn't properly understand the full name".

"Why should I care about this right now, Valentina? You just broke my heart"!

"Well not exactly. It was Joey who did. I'm just the bearer of bad news". Stefanie didn't reply. Her friend wasn't getting it. This was heartbreaking to her. She had really thought Joey was interested in her. Trying to process all the different thoughts that shot through her head, she said: "What is this apple supposed to be"?

"I don't know, but apparently Joey has been looking all over for it. That's why he looked so shabby at the restaurant where we met him. He goes out on these - for a lack of better words - treasure hunts".

"I see how it is. Let's go get this apple then", Stefanie decided. She was determined to find the relic, hoping this would score her points with Joey. Perhaps, they could still be together after all. Hope hadn't been lost completely and thus her mood lifted again. "How are you going to do that?", Valentina wanted to know. "Not sure. The room we're in looks like a library to me. We might find something on the apple in here", Stefanie suggested. "You're a genius. Let's do that", her friend agreed. With that, they started looking through all the different documents, papers, and books laying around. Trying to be careful, they made as little of a mess as possible. No one should conclude that the two girls had been snooping around.

Only a couple of minutes had passed by when Stefanie suddenly made a small shrieking noise. She had pulled out one of the books from the shelves. While skimming the pages, she fumbled upon something. Or rather, something had fallen out of the book. At first glance, it appeared to be a pamphlet of some sort but once Stefanie had picked up the peculiar object, she noticed that it was a map. It had been meticulously folded and obviously hidden within that book. Valentina had come to the same conclusion when she looked down on it. "Someone for sure did not want the general public to find this". The map was worn and faded and its sides were frayed and burned. Surprisingly, it was still in good condition, most likely because it had been made out of papyrus. Valentina was by no means a cartographer but she could tell that this map had to be at least a couple of centuries old. Her hunch was confirmed when she noticed a small number on the bottom right part, *refurbished Anno 1659*. The two girls put the map on the desk centered in the middle of the library. "This is a depiction of Milos", concluded Stefanie. Valentina nodded and with her fingers, she gently moved across the map. "This piece must have been in the possession of the Lewis family for decades", Valentina said, thinking out loud.

"What do you think is marked right here"?

Stefanie pointed to a small, dark red cross on the far east of the island.

"I have no idea but I'm sure this is where Joey wanders off to during the day. This must be the location of something important".

"We can't take it with us but let's take a picture".

Valentina quickly pulled out her phone and after climbing onto the leather chair, she took a picture of the whole map. "Put it back, so no one suspects a thing", Valentina ordered her friend. Meanwhile, she kept searching for clues. There must be something else. Something they were missing. The more time passed searching, the more anxious Stefanie suddenly became. She feared someone might walk in on them. "Don't worry, Joey is busy right now. No one will come", assured Valentina. Stefanie frowned. Thinking of Joey and Helena and what they were doing right now was beyond painful. "Oh my god! That's it!", Valentina suddenly exclaimed and ushered Stefanie to come over. She had opened a book that was laying on the desk. It had been right under her nose this whole time. "Listen to this... *The apple of Hephaestus* is believed to be an ancient relic. According to philosophers such as Socrates, Plato, and Homer, the apple is as old as the Greek gods. Legend has it that in ancient times, during the dawn of humanity, Hephaestus had molded and worked the apple out of pure honey, made from the healthiest bees. The honey had then fermented into solid gold. The relic had been requested by none other than *Narcissus*, the most beautiful man to ever walk the face of the earth. He had fallen in love with *Penelope*, a nymph and daughter of King Appolodorus. However, while the young man traveled to Penelope's residence, to deliver the gift and his desire for marriage, he made rest at a lake. There, he looked into the water and fell in love with his own beauty. With the apple in hand, he tried reaching for his reflection, just to fall into the lake and tragically drown. Centuries passed until the apple was discovered by Marco Polo, who then retrieved it, intending to bring the relic back to Venice. According to Donata Badoer's memoirs, her spouse got caught in a storm and stranded no place else than here on Milos. Apparently, Polo was then harassed by pirates and thus forced to hide the apple somewhere on the island. The only thing he left behind was this very map right here, saying that; *he who was worthy of possessing the apple would become its rightful owner*".

The two girls looked at each other in silence before Valentina added: "This is it! This is what Joey and Helena are after. The apple of Hephaestus".

"But it hasn't been found in centuries. I mean when was Polo alive? Thirteen-hundred something? That's why people don't believe in its existence anymore".

"Doesn't mean we can't find it. You do still want to score points with Joey, don't you"?

Stefanie nodded vehemently. Valentina wanted to say something when suddenly someone right outside their room said: "I haven't seen the two girls in a while". It was Monty, the butler. "Do you think they left already? Did they not enjoy my party?", replied Joey. He seemed genuinely disappointed. Apparently, their absence had been noticed. Paying attention to the men's footsteps, the two girls waited until the air had cleared out, before hushing out of the room.

SIX

"We need to go back! We're clearly missing something!", Valentina said excitingly. The two girls were back at their hotel. After sneaking out of Joey's library, the pair had quickly said their goodbyes and left for home. Much had to be discussed. Even though Valentina didn't want to, Joey had insisted his chauffeur drive them back. "This way I can be certain, you two beauties will make it home safe", he said with a big grin on his face. Stefanie was blushing, when he added ominously: "Milos can be dangerous at night". His efforts in sounding creepy failed miserably. The drive home was awkward, to say the least. Neither the driver nor the girls said a single word. Valentina didn't want the chauffeur to budge in on their conversation, possibly leaking to Joey that they too were now after the apple. They couldn't have gotten home fast enough. Valentina was burning to talk to Stefanie about what they had found in the reading room. And she could tell her friend was feeling the same way.

"How do you plan on getting back into his library though?", Stefanie asked. She had a good point.

Valentina had plenty of time to come up with a plan during their ride home. "I was pondering over that. How about you take Joey out for dinner, while I sneak into his house and look for more information?", she suggested.

"So... breaking and entering it is"?

"I wouldn't call it that. It's more like acquiring more data for our quest in winning Joey's love". Stefanie suddenly perked her ears. She was so gullible. "And, I was thinking, if you take him out to dinner, then you guys could come back to the hotel after for some fun. If you know what I mean. This would give me even more time to sweep the whole library". Valentina winked at her friend while saying that. Suddenly, Stefanie seemed very fond of this plan. The thought of her hooking up with Joey sounded very enticing. "But remember Stefanie, you must come back to the hotel. You cannot go back to his place"!

"What do I tell him if he asks about you"?

"Tell him I'm into star-gazing and that tonight is a good night to see a comet. That's also the reason why we rented a car and why I dropped you off. I'm using the car to go somewhere with as little artificial light as possible".

"And you think this plan will work"?

"It will. Just trust me on this one". Of course, Valentina's plan would work. Joey was too naive to suspect anything from his beautiful, innocent

Swiss friends. The thought of them tricking him would never even cross his mind.

The next day, while Stefanie was texting Joey inviting him out for dinner, Valentina went to rent another car. Later that day, the two girls got ready. Stefanie in a beautiful red dress to go out, Valentina in khakis to sneak into an estate. Halfway between the girls' hotel and Joey's grounds, the town of Kategea was situated. Stefanie and Joey had agreed upon meeting there. According to him, there was a beautiful, cozy restaurant overlooking the steppes laced with apple trees. After dropping off Stefanie and waving at an already waiting Joey, Valentina continued driving south. "Where is Valentina going?", asked Joey, as he led Stefanie onto the patio and to a table right by the railing. "She's very much into astronomy", explained Stefanie.
"Like the signs"?
"No. Like, observing stars and looking at planets".
"You can do that"?
"With the right equipment, certainly. Valentina has all sorts of telescopes and cameras".
"I didn't know". *Evidently*, thought Stefanie annoyed.

Valentina pulled up to the Lewis estate shortly after. She had parked her car further up the street right behind some trees, before making her way into the drive way. She felt as if she was in a mission-impossible movie. Pulling down a face mask early on so that cameras wouldn't detect her, she entered the premise and crouched over to the front door. There, she rang the bell before hurrying around the corner. As predicted, Monty came to open the door. She could hear him say loud and clear: "Hello? Is anyone there"? From where Valentina was lurking, she threw a pebble into a bush on the other side of the drive way. Monty, clearly unnerved, made his way over to check out the disturbance. Understanding that this was her moment, Valentina rushed to the veranda, where she silently opened the door and entered the mansion. Still crouched down, she made her way up to the library.

"It's starting to get late. Should we head home?", asked Joey. Stefanie and him had enjoyed some Lukumades. Essentially Greek mini-donuts. "You want to go home already? I was hoping to get a second dessert", she replied. Her thoughts went immediately to Valentina. She hadn't heard from her friend yet, even though Stefanie had gone to the bathroom multiple times to check her messages. Had Valentina already found what she was looking for? Was she in need of more time? *I'm sure she is*, Stefanie thought. Besides, Joey might not have been the smartest around, but he was still handsome and a woman had her cravings. "I always find space for an additional dessert", Joey smirked. "How about we go back to mine then?", Stefanie asked bluntly. All he did was nod and with that, the two left the restaurant.

Valentina knew she had been in the library for way too long. With a feeling of getting caught any second, she rushed from one end of the room to the other, incapable of finding what she was looking for. Joey had hidden his literary sources well. The map they had found, just wasn't enough to grasp an understanding of where the apple had been hidden. Getting frustrated, she flung one of the books from one side of the room to the other. What happened next baffled her greatly. A sort of sinking sound emanated. The type of noise that can be heard when a missing piece of artifact fits exactly into a pre-defined outlet, which then sets a whole mechanism into motion. Similarly, when Valentina threw a volume at the shelves across from her, it pushed a specific book further into the construction. Suddenly, the two mantelpieces moved outwards, before opening up and then driving vertically back into the wall, revealing a huge corkboard pampered with notes, articles, and a minutely detailed map of Milos. "Holy mother of god!", Valentina said in disbelief. She approached her finding quickly. It had made a huge ruckus, so she knew she had little time until someone would detect her. Dead-center on the board was a type-written riddle. It read:

Beneath the stage of ages past
Abundance lies dormant, safe at last
Awaiting one who solves the cast

"I can't believe it! This is the missing piece!", Valentina realized. She pulled out her phone and quickly took a close-up picture of the riddle, before photographing the whole wall as well. Afterward, she snuck out of the library. It was time to leave!

Meanwhile, a sweaty Joey got off Stefanie. "That was fantastic!", he said with a sigh of relief and pleasure. He was panting quite excessively. "It was", she returned. Stefanie had a sudden urge to pee, so she hushed out of bed and made her way over to the bathroom. There, she looked at herself in the mirror. What was she trying to do here? She loved Joey with all her heart and yet wished him death. Just looking at him made her unspeakably angry. But look at his face! He's adorable! What had she done to the world to be denied her well-deserved peace? He treated her nicely and said all the right things, but he didn't care for her. She was a mere toy to him. He didn't do her any good and she knew it. But what could she do? She loved him! They had spent the last hour or so making passionate love to each other. She was certain, he must love her now! She had given herself to him and her body was indeed a sight to behold. Surely, he had fallen for her now.

After she had crawled back into bed and his arms, he said: "It's nice spending time with someone so laid-back for once". Puzzled by his statement, she asked what he meant. "Helena is always on my heels about finding this stupid artifact. I mean don't get me wrong, it would help me financially a great deal too if I'd find it, but Helena is pushing me too much. She even threatened to get me assassinated by one of her hitmen. Can you believe that"?

"Hold on. You're telling me Helena is part of the Melian mafia"?

Clearly understanding he had said too much, he returned: "You haven't heard it from me".

"What do you mean by 'it could financially help you'"?

"My family's fortune has been lost, and I've been struggling to keep everything together for the past couple of years. If I could just find the apple of Hephaestus, I could use it to pull myself out of this financial crisis".

"I understand. What exactly is this apple?", she asked while caressing his chest.

"It's an ancient artifact. Apparently, it had been created by one of the Greek gods but was then lost somewhere here on the island. Both the Achillian Party and the Hectorian League are after it. Before you ask, they are two different fractions of a once-united Melian mafia. And then, there is me. Silly little Joey, the wannabe Indiana Jones, hoping to get to the apple before everyone else does, in an attempt to save his family's heritage". Stefanie stayed silent for a moment as she didn't know what to say at first. But then, she replied: "If you want, you could always come live with me in Switzerland".

"If the mafia doesn't kill me first", chuckled Joey.

"You can't die on me!", Stefanie pleaded and laid her head on his shoulder.

With a loud bang, the marble statue shattered on the ground. God curse her clumsiness! She had looked back over her shoulder because this sudden feeling of being watched had crept over her. "Master Lewis, is that you?", echoed Monty's voice from somewhere down the hall. Valentina had almost made it out of the mansion. Like the guard of a high-security prison, Monty did his rounds through the mansion. With a rusty old lantern, he walked down the hallways, ensuring no-one was around. Multiple times on her way out, Valentina had ducked behind a wall or ran into an open room to not get caught by the old man.

In the great hall, there sat an old telephone upon a wooden secretaire. When the butler was using it to call his master, Valentina was standing right around the corner, just millimeters away. Unable to reach anyone, Monty decided to walk back down the hall and enter the kitchen. It was during that moment when Valentina rushed out and knocked over the marble sculpture. She had already gone out onto the veranda when Monty re-appeared. Seeing nothing unusual, he once again returned to his midnight snack laying on the kitchen counter.

While Valentina crept hurriedly along the drive way and out of the estate, hostile eyes were watching her every move from behind a pulled-back curtain in one of the second-story rooms...

SEVEN

Dionisis Lagos was enjoying the mellow sensation of beautiful women. After another excruciating day of failing at figuring out how the murderer had gotten his hands on cyanide, he decided to do something different to get his mind off things. His trip out to the caves had not turned up anything. He had not found a single clue. Neither in Stefanie's demise nor in how she had gotten there. Lagos still had no idea on what she could have possibly wanted out there. Granted, the caves were a beautiful sight but why go there alone? Why was she there at night? How did she get there? There was no car, no bike, no nothing. She couldn't have possibly walked all the way from her hotel. And then there was the poison. How was she poisoned? By who, if not by herself? Whoever was responsible, how did they get their hands on cyanide? Clearly at his wit's end, he was fed up.

Lagos wanted to pass his time with something else for a change. Something worth living for. Having ordered multiple carafes of wine, Lagos was now in a great mood. At least he was supposed to. Stefanie's image haunted his every thought. Like running in a circle, he kept coming back to her. "Bring some food!", he ordered loudly. One of the women, a gorgeous red head from the main land, got up and went to the kitchen. It wasn't long before she placed a silver, oval bowl onto the table in front of Lagos. It was filled to the brim with fresh, ripe fruits. Apples, dates, figs, pomegranates, honey melons, and oranges were now adorning the table. Mindlessly reaching out from under the burial of women, he grabbed an apple. As he took a bite out of the juicy, red fruit, he suddenly stopped dead in his tracks. Clearly having a moment of enlightenment, he pushed one of the prostitutes off of him and then proceeded to rush over to his laptop. Butt-naked, he started punching in some words as if possessed. Upon finding whatever he was looking for, he shouted: "Heureka"!

Joey had left the hotel right around the same time as Valentina came back from her information hunt. The two had not crossed their ways in the lobby and so when she unlocked her room, she wasn't sure if her friend's lover would still be around. "What did you find?", Stefanie asked right as she came in the door. "A riddle", grinned Valentina. Her friend seemed greatly disappointed.
"What's with the long face"?
"I was hoping you'd find something more concrete".

"Well, that's only because you haven't heard yet where I've found it". And so, Valentina told her friend all about how she had retrieved the riddle and how she had to sneak out of the mansion. "You sound like James Bond".

"Kind of was", Valentina laughed. She felt self-assured.

"Let's see the riddle then"!

After reading it multiple times, Stefanie exclaimed: "What's that supposed to mean"? Valentina remained silent. She didn't know either. Getting annoyed with having to flick back and forth between the map and the riddle on her phone, she decided to write the conundrum down on a napkin. Afterward, she pulled up the picture of the map and laid it next to the paper. The two girls then leaned over both clues synchronously. "What could *beneath the stage of ages past* possibly mean?", Stefanie asked and scratched her head. "No idea. The movie theatre maybe?", Valentina returned in an effort to kick-start a brainstorming session.

The sun's last beams had vanished a long time ago when Valentina shouted: "Oh my god, Stefanie! We've found it! That's where the apple is hidden"! Excited and overtired, the two best friends grabbed each other's hands and started jumping around in a circle. They had finally done it. Hours of struggling with these abstract lines had passed, but they cracked it after all. "Let's go and get the apple right now!", proposed Stefanie in a frenzy.

"We're not in a hurry. Let's retrieve the relic tomorrow".

"Why, Valentina"?

"It's the middle of the night. It's dangerous right now. Tomorrow, during the day, we have decent light and can examine the whole thing properly".

"I think we should act right now".

"Let's not be hasty. No-one will steal it in the meantime. I mean, the apple has been presumed lost for decades now. What are the chances of someone finding it within the next six hours"?

"You're right, you're right! Fine, let's get to bed then", Stefanie gave in.

In her mind, however, she had already made other plans.

EIGHT

Darkness had befallen the island like a plague. The faint wind made shrubs shake lightly. Stefanie was shivering like a sick child when she made her way out of the hotel and into the night. She could hear the waves crash in on the beach ahead of her. The air was breezy. Nightfall had given the island a certain type of affront toward its inhabitants. As if hidden by mist, Stefanie got over from the hotel entrance to where the rental car was parked. She got in and swiftly turned on the engine. Flinching, as if she feared the noise would get her detected, she looked out of the window and up to where Valentina was sleeping. Nothing. Silence. Understanding that the coast was clear, she drove out of the parking lot and into the night.

During her drive, she kept thinking about Valentina. She felt bad for leaving her behind. They had agreed on retrieving the apple at daybreak, but this was too important. She had to get the relic before anyone else could. Every second mattered! What if Helena found the artifact first? Joey hadn't just slipped up about how the woman was pressuring him into finding the apple, but also how he had initially fallen in love with her. Stefanie needed to hand over the apple herself so he would want to be with her. She, the sweet girl, would restore his livelihood. For reasons she couldn't explain, Stefanie mistrusted Valentina lately. Stefanie knew her friend didn't want the apple for herself and was okay with giving it to Joey, but still, what if she would change her mind during the deliverance? What if she got greedy once seeing the beauty of the apple? Stefanie had to give the prized object to Joey. There was no other way of gaining his heart, even if it meant double-crossing her best friend in the process. She was sure, Valentina would understand. But why did she feel so bad? Valentina had been acting strange lately. Whenever Stefanie mentioned Joey, her friend would make a face as if she had just been struck by an invisible whip. Just hearing the man's name threw Valentina into a deep depression. At first, Stefanie didn't understand where her mood swings came from. Even now, they were a mystery to her but instead of wondering what she had done wrong, Stefanie just got annoyed. Why couldn't she just be happy for her? It wasn't Stefanie's fault Valentina had bad luck with men!

Completely immersed in her hateful thoughts toward her best friend, she almost missed her exit. Last minute, she was able to swerve onto the fork that got her off the freeway. Arriving at the top, she took a sharp right turn and then drove up an unlit, small country road. Checking Google maps multiple times along the way, Stefanie made sure she was on the right track.

Upon laying eyes on what appeared to be a great ruin on top of a hill in the darkness, Stefanie knew she had finally made it to her destination. On that raised plane, looking over Klima and the sea, towered an ancient theatre. Stefanie guessed it must've been built a couple hundred years before the turning of time. It was an imposing sight to behold. Built out of pure marble and still in good condition, it had to have been the meeting point of numerous generations past. The theater had certainly served as a showplace for countless performances and plays such as Antigone by Sophocles, Hamlet by Shakespeare to more contemporary pieces like The Lion King. Stefanie parked her car on the side of the road before getting out and starting the ascend up to the monumental sight. If deciphered correctly, the apple's location must've been somewhere around here.

Panting heavily, she eventually made it up to the theatre. It was so dark, she could barely see her own hands. She quickly pulled out her phone and turned on the flashlight. In doing so, she realized where she was. She stood in a large, oval arena. The ground had been paved with marble stones. On the right side of the wall stood a large wooden stand. This had to be the stage. The wall behind it had large hole-like windows. If one were to sit in the grandstand of stones across, one could look out into the sea during the performances. *What a breathtaking sight*, Stefanie thought. She made her way across and started looking around. Stefanie wasn't sure what she was trying to find but just something, anything to indicate where the apple was possibly hidden. Paying close attention to everything, she first scoured the wooden stand. But to no avail. Stefanie then decided to look for clues along the walls and lastly on the grandstand. She noticed immediately, how much higher the first row was built from the rest. At first, she thought this must've been done to lift the spectators so that even the ones at the bottom could have a good look at the stage. But then, she noticed something. There was a small, almost golden stone, worked right into the center of this wall. "Here goes nothing", Stefanie said to herself before pushing the stone inwards. With an ear-deafening rumble, a door-sized piece of the wall, right next to the golden stone, suddenly started moving into the stalls, before then shifting right and vanishing completely, leaving behind the entrance to a tomb. While the dust of ancient times fell from the ceiling, Stefanie stood there amazed by her finding. This was it! This must've been the entrance to an underground sanctuary of some sort. Collecting all of her courage and checking the battery left on her phone, Stefanie entered the narrow hallway.

Right outside, hidden behind the steering wheel of a car, prying eyes were watching her.

Stefanie made her way further down into the tomb. Cobwebs repeatedly smacked her face and slowly but surely she started to get anxious. The tunnel appeared to be getting narrower. What if she got stuck? The thought of her suffocating or starving to death was horrifying. Fighting her thoughts, she pressed on. Then, finally, after what felt like an eternity she entered a small chamber. Just like the rest, it had been constructed out of solid stone. With a mere twenty feet in diameter, the room was tiny. A skeleton lay in the right corner. On its skull, a gigantic spider rested. It didn't bother Stefanie too much, as her attention was fully drawn toward what lay ahead of her. There, in the ground, was a flight of stairs leading further down into complete darkness. She was scared to death. What could possibly be down there? Deciding it was too late to return now, she started descending. With trembling knees, she took one step after the other. Upon getting to the bottom of the stairs, she continued on and soon after walked into another bigger chamber. Unlike the rest of the creepy tomb, this space was gorgeous to look at. From the tiny light of her flashlight, she could tell that the room had been laced with gold. Beautiful drawings of Greek gods had been worked into the layer of minerals. Slowly scanning the room, Stefanie's gaze fell upon what looked like a sanctuary. She approached it. On it lay gorgeous, dried flowers and fruits. And then, Stefanie saw it. Dead center, neatly nested upon an arrangement of purple silk, lay the apple of Hephaestus. It glimmered in the faint light of her phone. Roughly double the size of a regular apple, it looked just like the fruit. Touching it made Stefanie realize how smooth its surface was. She had done it! She had found the apple!

Stefanie suddenly made an incisive decision. She would leave the apple behind and secretly return later with Joey. Why take away the artifact from here? She could lose it on the way, or drop it and thus break the relic. Instead, she could just bring the love of her life here and have him take the risk of carrying the apple. After all, no one would come to steal it. She was the only one in the entire world who knew how to get to it. Not even Valentina knew. Stefanie held all the power by herself. Pleased with her work and confident in her decision, she quickly turned and left the tomb.

Meanwhile, the prying eyes waited patiently. Understanding what must've happened, they drove off. Someone had to be informed about this.

NINE

When Valentina woke up the next morning, Stefanie was peacefully sleeping next to her. With her brown hair and red, full lips she was beautiful to look at. Just the proximity of her presence lit an indistinguishable fire in Valentina's heart. Trying hard not to wake her best friend, she got dressed and went out of the room. Casually, neither thinking nor worrying about anything, she took the elevator down to the lobby. From there she went out into the yard where she had breakfast. It was a beautiful garden with all sorts of flowers in full bloom. The air was filled with sweet and rich flavors. The buzzing of bees could be heard clearly. The water of a fountain in the shape of an angel splashed continuously. It stood in the center of the garden surrounded by small hedges. Today was a lovely day.

Valentina was eating a croissant while reading the morning paper, when Stefanie walked out of the lobby and over to her table. The two greeted each other. "Are you alright?", Valentina asked. Stefanie looked drained. Her friend had put a hefty amount of makeup on, but Valentina could see past the facade.

"I'm fine. I just couldn't sleep very well".

"Did you have nightmares"?

"Something of the sort, yes". Stefanie looked beaten down but Valentina didn't want to push it any further. If her friend didn't want to talk about it, then that was her decision to make. An awkward silence filled the air, or least, that's how Valentina perceived it. Afterward though, she couldn't remember any more if it actually had been that way or if she had just imagined it. Maybe Stefanie was completely fine with the situation. "Are you ready to go find the apple?", Valentina asked to change the topic and breathe some air into her friend. "About that. I don't know if we should go look for it after all", Stefanie reckoned.

"Why not"?

"What's the point? It's not our job to find it. We know where it is, but that doesn't mean the rest of the world has to. Especially not Joey".

"That's not true! What's wrong with you, Stef? I thought you wanted to present him the apple in an effort to demonstrate your undying love"?

"I don't think laying the world at his feet will ever make him love me"!

"Why would you say such a thing"? Valentina looked at her best friend worriedly. "Like you ever cared!", Stefanie snapped, before adding: "Never mind. I'm meeting someone later, so if you could stay here, I'd appreciate it". After dropping such an aggressive statement, she got up. She hadn't touched a single item of her breakfast. A hurt and confused Valentina remained seated at the table.

Deeply immersed in her thoughts, Stefanie left the hotel. She got into the rental car and drove off. She was on a mission. Stefanie didn't look back once. Hence, she also didn't notice Valentina running out of the lobby, right as she swirled out of there. It was easier to do it this way. Having found the apple put the two of them in extreme danger. From what they knew, both the mafia and the police could be after them now. By kicking Valentina out of the boat and forcing her to swim, Stefanie would be the only one drowning with this sinking ship. She did it for her best friend because deep down she knew she loved her. Driving along the ocean side, a tear fell from her cheek.

When she arrived at the restaurant, her date was already waiting. Sitting comfortably on a wide, red cushioned chair sat Helena Kostea. Elegantly dressed in a black, tight dress with matching heels, she had one leg over the other while leaning over the back of the chair. She might have had sunglasses on, but it was clear that she was watching Stefanie intently as she entered. "Hello Stefanie", spoke the seated one with an air of brutal coldness. "Helena", greeted Stefanie back. She was intimidated by her counterpart but she tried to hide it as best as she could. The two of them were not on particularly good terms anymore. What had started as an amicable friendship soon turned into a bitter rivalry. Their common point of contention was none other than Joey Lewis. Or at least, that's what Stefanie thought. The two of them had exchanged phone numbers during Joey's party and soon after started chatting. Helena showed great courteousness and even offered to show the two girls around the island accompanied by her personal bodyguard. What seemed like an offer coming from a place of deep care, was actually a surveillance act. Helena wanted to watch them. Keep them at arm's length, making sure they could not intervene with her daily business. Essentially, Helena wanted to keep Stefanie busy so she couldn't spend as much time with Joey. That was Stefanie's conviction. On one occasion, when Helena intended to have the girls driven to a local food market for the day, the two friends refused. When they explained to Helena that they had other plans, she was deeply infuriated. This prompted her to send inappropriate text messages to Stefanie. From then on, she knew that Helena wasn't actually a friend but rather a foe. It got especially dire when Valentina nudged Stefanie one day in Adamantas to let her know that they were being followed. And sure enough, when she turned around, a woman hurriedly looked away and acted as if she had just dropped something. The two best friends had differing opinions on why Helena behaved the way she did. Stefanie was convinced she tried keeping them away from Joey. Valentina on the other hand, thought she was watching them in case they got to the apple of Hephaestus first. It was with the belief of Helena sheltering Joey, that Stefanie agreed upon meeting her enemy. She was here to fight for her lover. Backed up with the knowledge of the apple's location, she was certain to have one up on Helena. Now, the time had come to tell her rival to back off. All cards would be laid out on the table today.

After some absurdly shallow small talk, Helena ordered them penne alla vodka. Accompanying the dish was a white wine produced locally. "This is my favorite", Helena smiled. After taking a sip, Stefanie agreed upon its deliciousness. After some more chit-chatter, Stefanie excused herself to head the restroom. She spent roughly five minutes in there before returning to Helena. "I'm glad you suggested this meeting", said Stefanie as she began her frontal attack, "I've been meaning to talk to you about something".

"And what would that be"?

"This is about my one true love. It's about Joey. You really think you can keep me from being with him"?

Helena remained silent, staring intently at her counterpart. Meanwhile, Stefanie was borderline chugging her wine. The pasta had made her ridiculously thirsty.

"You think... you can... keep me... he and I are... meant for each...".

Stefanie did not know what was happening to her. Suddenly, she felt a burdensome dizziness. She was so tired, she could hardly finish her sentence. Hell, she could not even organize her thoughts properly. "What you're trying to say is; you're meant for each other?", spoke Helena to help get her friend's message across. While doing so, she leaned in as if she was trying to better understand. "Yeaaah...", was all Stefanie could mumble at that point. Helena started giggling. It was a mean, sort of looking down on her, laugh. Stefanie was incapable of answering. Her head was spinning. She could barely see Helena. She felt warm and sleepy. This wasn't good! "You're here because of Joey? Oh, you poor girl! How completely foolish of you!", laughed Helena. A look of mad perturbation had wandered across her face. Those devilishly, crazed eyes were the last thing Stefanie saw. Before passing out, she could hear Helena say:

"If it's him you want; you can have the man-whore"!

TEN

The sun was setting on Milos in hues of dark-orange, red, and pink. Crickets chirped in complete contentment across the island and into the world. What felt like divine peacefulness was all but a mirage. The island was on edge. Three days had passed since the tragic death of Stefanie Sigmund and so far, no one had been made responsible. The people demanded justice. Two persons on the island, however, couldn't care less. Helena Kostea and Joey Lewis were on their way to ascend the stairs up to the ancient theatre. From their research, they had finally located the apple of Hephaestus. That was all that mattered right now. Who cared about what the poverty on the island was screaming about? The two of them were about to become richer than the gods themselves. "Are you really sure this is it?", asked Joey while heaving himself up the steep steps. "I'm positive", Helena said. "How do you know?", he asked once they had reached the top.

"I have my sources. Just trust me on this one".

"I always trust you", he said and kissed her. "Okay, let's keep going then", she urged him. She seemed oddly stressed and on edge today. Normally, Helena was the more relaxed in their relationship. Joey brushed it off. It was probably just her excitement to find the apple. They had spent years on this. Her enthusiasm was understandable. "The entry must be around here somewhere. Just keep looking", Helena ordered him. "Come check this out! I think I've found something", he shouted after a little while. She practically ran over to him from the wooden stage. It was a golden stone, slightly elevated from the rest of the wall upon which the spectator ranks lay. "What are you waiting for? Push the thing!", she pressured him.

"What if it makes the whole theatre collapse"?

"Stop being silly! Just press it"!

He did as told. With a loud rumble, a door-sized part of the wall started moving into the ranks and then shifted aside to expose a passageway. "Holy mother of god", exclaimed Joey. "You did it! You've found the entrance to where the apple must be hidden!", Helena said with a gleam of excitement in her eyes. She was pumped! Fortune and wealth were in arms reach. "What are you waiting for?", she asked him. Clearly frightened but wanting to be the man, he stepped into the narrow passage.

The two of them made it through an endless-seeming hallway of complete darkness. Their small little flashlights barely did anything to suggest what could possibly lie ahead. Joey held Helena by her hand. She didn't quite know why. There was nothing to trip over. And they couldn't get lost either. The only way was to go forward. Finally, after what felt like ages, the two of them made it into a tiny chamber with nothing in it but a skeleton and a flight of stairs, inviting them to go further down. The two of them looked at each other wearily. "Go on…", Helena nudged. Hesitating for a moment, Joey obliged. Helena followed him closely. When they got to the bottom of the stairs, they found themselves in a large chamber set in pure gold. At the back end, neatly nested in-between dried fruits and upon purple satin sat the apple of Hephaestus. Even in the dim light, the surface of the relic was flashing all across the room. Joey quickly rushed forward to grab the apple, when suddenly he felt an excruciating pain go through his body. Not just once, but threefold did it strike his back at intervals of one fraction of a second each time. A loud, ear-deafening bang accompanied each shock. Falling to the ground, he turned around. To his disturbance, he saw Helena holding a raised, still smoking gun. She had shot him! Without either of them saying a single word, he watched her as she stepped over him and snatched the apple from its socket. Helena stayed silent as a ghost until she reached the stairs, where she suddenly turned around. "What are you doing?", he hissed at her in pain. He was confused and angry. With startling calmness and as if explaining something to a toddler, she said: "Do you really think you could betray me and I wouldn't find out"? Confused as to what she was speaking of, he remained silent. "Poor Joey, really thought he could play Stefanie against me. Remember when you came knocking at my door in the middle of the night? You told me that the little Swiss nuisance had taken the apple, but here it is, completely untouched. You tried to cross me behind my back, so I had to double-cross you", explained Helena, not once looking away from the bleeding mess in front of her. "You can't do this!", he pleaded, "I have always been loyal to you. This is a misunderstanding"! "Try telling that to the gods. You'll be meeting them soon", and with that, she started for the stairs. Right when she got out of sight, she turned around and shouted down to Joey: "This is what you get for cheating on me and then trying to backstab me. The apple belongs to me! It always has! Have fun rotting down here". She hurriedly ran up the remaining two steps, quickly turned around, and shot repeatedly at the ceiling right above. With a loud rumble, the whole thing imploded, burying Joey's desperate screams forever.

With an air of victory and holding the apple tightly to her chest, Helena walked back up the passageway to the entrance. With her heart pounding, she pushed the golden stone on her left to kick-start the gate mechanism. She then moved a few steps back to let the door do its thing.

Afterward, she walked through the opening, just to be greeted by Inspector Lagos holding his gun dead-center at her face. "Drop the weapon and hand me the apple! Now, move away from the entrance!", he ordered her calmly. Since she had entered the sanctuary, nightfall had settled. The stars were shining down on Helena silently obeying. "You will regret this!", she said, clearly out of place to make such a statement. With his eyebrows risen, Lagos watched as Selim appeared behind Helena and handcuffed her. Inspector Lagos then spoke: "Helena Kostea, I hereby charge you with the murder of Stefanie Sigmund and the attempted murder of Joey Lewis"! At the same time, Valentina crested the stairs of the theatre and walked in on the scene. She had heard Lagos accusing Helena of her best friend's murder. "So you really did it?", she asked disbelievingly after being close enough. Shock was written all over her face. "You can't prove anything!", Helena interrupted arrogantly before spitting on Lagos' shoes. Without the slightest warning, Selim punched her in the side of the head with a clenched fist. "Show some respect!", he shouted at her, as Helena crashed against the wall behind her before falling to the ground. Meanwhile, Valentina was on the verge of crying. Selim had pulled out his gun and was now pointing it directly at a nose-bleeding Helena. "You want proof? Let me provide it to you", Lagos started his monologue, "You murdered Ms.

Sigmund because she found the apple of Hephaestus before you did. You had to get rid of her because, unlike you, she didn't want to keep the relic but instead hand it over to Mr. Lewis. She thought if she could give him the prized object, he would fall in love with her. Out of sheer gratitude, I assume. If I'm not mistaken, Ms. Zehnder you were okay with that, right"? Valentina nodded vehemently before asking: "How did Helena know we were after the apple"?

"That is a very good question! And I can give you the answer to that. It was Ms. Kostea watching you leave the Lewis estate after you retrieved that riddle", Lagos explained. "How do you know?", inserted the accused herself. "Talked to Monty, the butler. He told me Mr. Lewis was hosting you that night. If it is true that the old man was busy eating a sandwich in the kitchen, you are the only plausible solution to this. I reckon, after being pulled out of your sleep from hearing the bookshelves move, you quickly made your way to the library, where you saw Ms. Zehnder taking a picture of the riddle. You watched, as she left the grounds", Lagos said. The inspector interpreted her silence as an affirmation. "Ms. Kostea, from that moment on, you knew this would be a race against time. That's why you had the girls watched by your goonies. Unfortunately for Ms. Sigmund, she didn't quite apprehend why she was being followed. You see, she thought you wanted to keep her away from

Mr. Lewis", Lagos continued his revelation. "She was blatantly gullible from the beginning", interrupted Helena scoffingly. Overhearing her statement, Lagos continued: "You knew you had to get rid of Ms. Sigmund when Mr. Lewis told you she had found the relic". "Joey did what? How?", Valentina was stunned.

Lagos explained: "It was none other than Mr. Lewis who watched Ms. Sigmund on the night she supposedly retrieved the apple. He was observing her from his car, as she ascended up to the theatre just to then vanish into the tomb of Hephaestus. But he drove off too early, not witnessing how the girl left the apple behind". Here, Lagos made a theatrical pause to let his statement sink in. "How do you know?", Valentina inquired. "Again, the butler... Ms. Zehnder, do you remember the party Mr. Lewis hosted on his estate? I was there. I was one of the attendees. I talked to Monty during the event. From him, I was told that Mr. Lewis and Ms. Kostea were working together to find the apple. You see, Ms. Kostea, Monty is an old friend of mine. He used to work for the Hectorian League so he had no issue telling me all he knew. From that social gathering on, I had all of you tailed by my men. On the night Ms. Sigmund found this sanctuary right here, I was parked just a couple of meters behind Mr. Lewis. I saw everything. From how she ascended the stairs to him driving off", Lagos smirked. "Monty is a traitor!", shouted Helena. "Not at all. He is simply a man of old traditions. See, Mr. Lewis' dad is the founding father of the Hectorian League while his mother would later on establish the Achillian Party. Monty had always served both sides. According to him, the mafia is still one big family", corrected Lagos. Helena was speechless by this revelation.

"Back to what I was initially talking about. Accordingly, the night you, Ms. Zehnder, and Ms. Sigmund deciphered the riddle, instead of going to bed, Ms. Sigmund went out to the ancient theatre. She wanted to find the apple immediately before making her way to Joey. I'm not quite sure yet why she did what she did, but she must've had her reasons. Either way and more importantly, there was a big misunderstanding between Mr. Lewis and Ms. Kostea".

"What do you mean by that?", Helena asked.

"You see, Ms. Kostea, unlike what you thought, Mr. Lewis didn't want to betray you, but instead double-cross Ms. Sigmund. He had always been loyal to you. The only mistake he made was to take off too early. With his leaving too soon, he didn't see Ms. Sigmund return to the surface empty-handed. If he had waited, he would've known she had left the apple behind".

"Why had she done that?", Valentina wanted to know.

"I suppose, she wanted to take him to the location in person, not deliver the artifact like some post owl".

"But Inspector, when I woke up she was sleeping right next to me. Why didn't Stefanie go directly to Joey the night she found the apple"?

"She did, but no one was home! Remember, Mr. Lewis was at Ms. Kostea's at the same time. Disappointed, but convinced of catching her lover the next day, Ms. Sigmund returned to her hotel. Monty once again serves as proof. After all, it was he who opened up the door to her that fateful night".

"So you're telling me, if Joey had returned home instead of going to Helena's, this whole thing wouldn't have happened"?

"Pretty much", Lagos said, shrugging his shoulders.

"Wait! Why"? Helena asked. She was furious about her confusion.

"Simple! If Mr. Lewis had driven home instead of coming to you, he would've encountered Ms. Sigmund. She would've told him all about the apple and together they would have retrieved the artifact. She would've willingly handed over the apple to him. He would've either fled the island with or without her.

If he hadn't come to you, Ms. Kostea, then you would've never learned of Ms. Sigmund's finding the apple, and thus there would've never been a need to murder her. There would have never been the need to double-cross Mr. Lewis either, because he would've probably vanished with the apple by now.

Essentially, you're going to jail for nothing, and with nothing". After saying that, Lagos was grinning with the confidence of a man who had just put his opponent in checkmate.

"You still haven't proven a single thing!", Helena shouted stubbornly.

"Are you sure? I'm pretty positive you know what this is", Lagos countered and pulled a small glass jar out of his pocket. In it was a dark powdery substance. "I found this at your house", he continued. Helena looked angry. "Apart from that, do you know why I know you did it? Primarily because, on the day Ms. Sigmund disappeared, she was last seen having lunch with you, Ms. Kostea. I have multiple witnesses stating they saw you mix something in her food at the restaurant. And here is where it gets interesting. I know *how* you murdered her. You mixed finely ground apple seeds into her dish", Lagos explained, "because this is it right here". While saying that, he shook the little jar. "How do you know what the powder is?", Helena asked. She was stunned. "See, when one pulverizes the seeds of an apple, they release a toxin called cyanide.

Cyanide is extremely lethal in large amounts. You knew how to make it because you, my dear, are a medical doctor. I searched the whole island, and not a single licensed practitioner holds even one drug containing cyanide or the powder itself. It must've been produced by someone with the knowledge. Having this realization, my thoughts circled in on you. And sure enough, when I searched your place, I found exactly what I was looking for.

What I can't believe though, is how mind-numbingly obvious you proceeded, Ms. Kostea. My god, the apple was right in front of me this entire time. I mean, just look around you, there are apple trees everywhere on this island. It was the simplest thing to do". Lagos started laughing in disbelief as he said that. "Either way, let's bring this big revelation back to how you murdered Ms. Sigmund. See, the amount of cyanide you mixed into her food wasn't actually enough to kill her. Instead, it just made her pass out. That is exactly what happened after you had dragged her to your car and drove off", Inspector Lagos continued. Interrupting him, Helena said: "Wait! So you're saying...".

"Exactly. When you tossed Ms. Sigmund into the caves, she was still alive, just unconscious. In the end, too weak to fight, the poor girl drowned down there. Abandoned by her friends and alone, naked the way she had entered the world in the first place".

Valentina started crying, overcome by the news of her best friend's horrifying death. Even Helena fell into silence. She had mixed the toxin into Stefanie's food because she wanted to give her a quick death. The girl, perhaps not the brightest, was still a sweet enough soul to deserve a quick and painless death. "So she double-crossed Joey out of greed?", Selim asked. "No. See, once Mr. Lewis had told her that Ms. Sigmund found the apple, Ms. Kostea went to the sanctuary to find out for herself if what he was saying was true. Our Ms. Kostea right here is a very mistrusting person after all. Finding the apple completely untouched in the golden chamber led her to believe that Mr. Lewis had lied to her and that he had secretly switched sides. She thought it best to then simply eliminate the both of them", Lagos elaborated. "That was right before she went to meet Stefanie at the restaurant?", Valentina asked to make sure she stayed on track with the timeline. "Right on, Ms. Zehnder. But it gets better! This apple right here", Lagos said and threw the apple slightly up in the air before catching it again, "is actually a fake". And with that, he flung the relic at the wall where it shattered into a thousand pieces. Everyone was shocked, all but Helena. "You bastard!", she laughed. "Ms. Kostea, correct me if I'm wrong, but you had the real apple on you when you went to meet Ms. Sigmund at the restaurant. In fact, you didn't just throw the poor girl into the Papafragas caves but the relic too. Your plan was to retrieve it there, once you were done dealing with Mr. Lewis", Lagos smirked.

"To summarize it all", he continued, "Understanding that Ms. Sigmund had deciphered the riddle before everyone else did, made her a threat big enough to be eliminated. She knew she could retrieve the apple at any point and thus you, Ms. Kostea, thought it best to get rid of her. Being aware that the apple was still at the sanctuary, you believed Mr. Lewis and Ms. Sigmund were on the same team now. Thus, you decided that both of them had to die. First, you took care of Ms. Sigmund by inviting her out to lunch where you drugged her before throwing her naked into the caves to drown. It was there, you also hid the apple. Afterward, you burned her clothes to leave no traces of your own DNA. Then, you led Mr. Lewis to believe the apple must've been lost where Ms. Sigmund was found because according to him she had the apple, right? And that's how I saw you two climb up from the caves yesterday. Apparently unable to find the relic there, you convinced Mr. Lewis that he had to decipher the riddle before leading him here. During all of it, you acted as if you didn't know the location of the tomb of Hephaestus already. You then double-crossed the trusting man and left him to die. And so, here we are now. Have I missed anything"?

"You made one tiny mistake, yes. We never deciphered the riddle! We knew it had to be nearby, based on Joey's observations during the night Stefanie discovered the entrance.", Helena confessed, "Tell me the riddle's solution! It's been tormenting me for ages now".

"Certainly", Lagos agreed,

"Beneath the stage of ages past,

Abundance lies dormant, safe at last,

Awaiting one who solves the cast.

The stage of ages past is referring to the ancient theatre. The symbolism of the apple and evidently Milos, is *abundance*, which also refers to the apple of Hephaestus. In other words, abundance is a metaphor for the relic. Just like you created cyanide from the most obvious fruit on the island Ms. Kostea, in his riddle Marco Polo referred to the most frequently occurring thing on Milos... the apple tree. *Awaiting one who solves the cast* means that whoever can see past complete obviousness will find his treasure", Lagos explained. Helena started laughing. It was a sad laugh. Understanding the complete shallowness of it all, made her feel enormously terrible about murdering an innocent tourist and trying to kill the love of her life as well. Slowly but surely, her laugh started to turn into tears. While Selim escorted her to his car, heavy tears were falling from her cheeks. "Ms. Zehnder, please go wait with the police officer. I must make efforts to find Mr. Lewis", Lagos urged her. He then vanished into the sanctuary while Valentina followed Selim's tail. After aggressively throwing a churned-up Helena onto the backseat, Selim proceeded to call first responders. Soon after, Lagos approached the car, carrying Joey over his shoulder. The man was pale and could barely even stand up straight. He must've lost a lot of blood. After taking care of Joey and briefly talking to Lagos, Selim drove off to prison. Meanwhile, Valentina and Lagos waited and watched as first responders sped up the hill. Their sirens echoed across the whole island. Before the cars arrived and without looking at Valentina once, Lagos asked: "You loved her, didn't you"? He did so with an empathy no-one ever expected from a rough man such as his kind. "I did. Oh god, I really did! With all my heart", Valentina broke down. She started crying. Finally, she was able to let loose of everything.

It gave her a feeling of relief.

EPILOGUE

An unexpectedly chilly wind blew on the morning after Helena's arrest. It felt like autumn had set in sooner than usual. As if the island was mourning the tragedy that had unfolded only a couple of hours ago. Inspector Dionisis Lagos was on his way out to the Papafragas caves. Looking down, he could see the now dark-green water moving back and forth. Almost like an old man in his rocking chair. Carefully, and with the help of Akis Marakos, he descended into the cave with a rope tied around his waist. "Can you see anything?", shouted the old farmer from above. "Not yet, Akis. Let me slide down further", replied Lagos. Strained, he looked around him, hoping to see a glimmer somewhere. He was about to give up hope when suddenly, something began to glitter in the shadow of a hollow in front of him. Lagos quickly realized that this must be the apple of Hephaestus. "Hold on tight, Akis", he shouted up in hopes of the other hearing him. Then, he started swinging from one end of the cave to the other. On his third attempt, he was able to grab hold of one of the rocks. Painfully he managed to pull himself in and retrieve the apple. It lay heavy in his hand when he told the old farmer to pull him back up.

"What are you going to do with it, Inspector?", smiled Akis as they looked upon the shimmering relic together. "What I have promised my father a long time ago. I will restore our great nation and bring an end to this devastating economic depression. Have the Greeks live in prosperity once more", the inspector replied. Akis smiled at him in an approving manner. Lagos' thoughtful gaze on the apple quickly turned into a hearty laugh, when he added:

"But first, let me get back to the only two things every man must truly love; wine and women".

While the two old men walked gaily to their respective vehicles, Helena was violently thrown into a prison cell. They had forced her to stand outside the police station the entire night. An angry mob of onlookers had come by and thrown old vegetables at her. The communities on the island were deeply disturbed by what she had done. Now, the once most beautiful woman on the whole island reeked of urine and rotten vegetables. She could barely move a muscle and so she lay there, on the hard, cold stone floor. Her physical pain was nothing compared to what she felt on an emotional level. Stefanie Sigmund was haunting her every thought. Deep regret for what she had done twitched through her body like shockwaves. She had begged for forgiveness. She had begged for Zeus to strike her down so violently as she had done with Stefanie. But, Helena wasn't heard. This was her divine punishment. Whenever her brain wasn't completely absorbed with Stefanie, it hushed over to Joey. She didn't know how he was, or where he was, or if he was even alive. "Forgive me...", Helena said faintly to herself. A tear fell from her rosy but dirty cheek.

Meanwhile, Joey Lewis was sitting on the patio of his estate. Sad and beaten down he looked out into the gardens of his family manor. He had been sent home after being quickly patched up together. Joey had insisted so. He wanted Monty to take care of him rather than some unemotional nurse. Mindlessly observing the waves out front clashing against the rocks separating his estate from the sea, he understood that all had been lost. With Helena in prison and the apple in Lagos' hands, there was nothing he could do to prevent the inevitable downfall of his family's legacy. He would have to sell the house and inadvertently his soul. Joey would have to move back to Britain. A country that was more foreign to him than anything else in the world. But all of that didn't matter. Neither his defeat in this fight for the apple nor the heartbreaking betrayal of his lover really meant anything to him. First and foremost, he was mourning Stefanie's tragic death and its uselessness. This thought, being the primary reason for her death, made his throat feel like a knot. He had done her wrong, and there was nothing he could do to bring her back. As he looked at one of the withered flowers laying in front of his feet, he silently wished to be dead too.

While Joey was drowning in his own thoughts, Valentina Zehnder boarded a plane. It was time to go home. To leave behind this island and all the dark memories attached to it. Deeply mourning the death of her beloved friend, she felt dreary about what would await her in Switzerland. After all, she would have to return to their shared apartment. A place where everything reminded her of Stefanie. Her one true love. She sat down in one of the window seats at the backend of the airplane. Valentina couldn't help but cry when she looked out into the scenery. Grey clouds hung deep in the sky. The wind was blowing leaves and tiny bushes across the meager mountains. A light rain had begun to drum against her window. It seemed as if the gods were crying too. It bore little condolence for her. Never in her life would she forget her best friend's memory. Her smile. Her dark-brown, caring eyes. Her smell of lavender and citrus. Her vibrant, deeply touching personality. Stefanie had been a miracle, and she had been taken out of this life way too early. Wherever she was now, Valentina truly hoped it was a better place. A place where someday, they would meet again.

There was much to be talked about...

A special thank you to Debbie, my editor

DOLOR

1946, New York

Tom, a charming and ambitious young man, embarks on a promising career at the New York Police Department. Alongside his thriving personal life, he encounters the enchanting Emily at his closest friend's wedding, leading them to fall deeply in love.

Yet, as Tom's career flourishes, he becomes entangled in a series of perplexing and seemingly unsolvable murders. Additionally, the rise in influence of a menacing gang poses a significant threat, potentially shattering Tom's glamorous path. The supposed loss of his beloved Emily could push him to the brink of his mental stability, a place engulfed by nothing but shadows and despair.

CURRENTLY ONLY AVAILABLE IN GERMAN

TIMUR E. SIMSEK

Timur E. Simsek lives in Bern, Switzerland. Most of his childhood was spent reading fiction or crafting short stories. At the age of twenty-three he issued his first novel *dolor*. His other interests include history, Greek mythology, and cultural studies. He recently graduated from the University of Applied Sciences in Bern and plans on pursuing a master's degree in the near future.

dilitirio is his second publication and his first novella.